maximalismo

lismo

maximalism

lismo

maximalismo

maximalismo

alism

maximalismo

maximalism

ismo

极繁主义建筑设计

maximalism
极繁主义建筑设计

maximalism
极繁主义建筑设计

Loft Publications

陕西师范大学出版社

图书在版编目（CIP）数据

极繁主义建筑设计／帕科·阿森修，奥罗拉·奎托著；成华鑫译.
—西安：陕西师范大学出版社，2004.5
ISBN 7-5613-2942-3

Ⅰ.极… Ⅱ.①帕… ②成… Ⅲ.建筑设计—世界—图解 Ⅳ. TU206

中国版本图书馆 CIP 数据核字（2004）第 029931 号

图书代号：SK4N0468

版权登记证号／陕版出图字：25-2004-037 号

Maximalism

Editor：Paco Asensio

Author：Aurora Cuito

Copyright holder of the original edition：

2003 © LOFT Publications S.L.

双子座丛书

总策划／黄利 万夏

图文编辑／刘晓燕

极繁主义建筑设计

帕科·阿森修 奥罗拉·奎托／著

成华鑫／译

责任编辑／周宏

出版发行／陕西师范大学出版社

经销／新华书店

印刷／北京国彩印刷有限公司

版次／2004 年 5 月第 1 版

2004 年 5 月第 1 次印刷

开本／880×1230 毫米 1/24 7 印张

字数／28 千字

书号／ISBN 7-5613-2942-3／J·52

定价／58.00 元（全二册）

 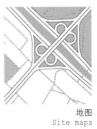  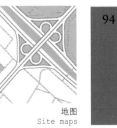

繁复永无停歇

历史上的各个艺术运动呈周期性地在繁华与简朴之间摇摆。这种在繁复与简单之间往复的趋势最早可以在罗马和哥特艺术的比较中看到：罗马艺术受一种难以理解的技艺驱使，生出简单与纯净的形式；而哥特艺术则由于建筑体系的进步，造出复杂得多的几何图形。

这种趋势在随后的艺术运动中一再地重复着，例如简单的古典线条向装饰主义与巴洛克的相互融合转变，在建筑物上堆砌了复杂的螺旋花样、翅梁、裙板和檐口。同样，进入20世纪后，领先于后现代主义的现代化运动致力于形式与材料的简化，而在后现代主义时期，建筑的直角消失，几何元素变得复杂，显示出丰富多变的效果。90年代初期简约主义的诞生意味着循环的又一轮更替，它是一种在内容繁复的后现代主义与解构主义之后出现的寻求缓冲的风格，这种追逐简单的倾向发展为一种热潮，创作者和客户都充分接受了这种将白色、直角和设计手段的精妙发挥到极致的潮流。回应这种无所不在的状态，一种新的艺术创作体系出现了，反映出人们对于较复杂的艺术形式的需求。在以下的建筑之中，客户和设计者们都想重新创造他们需求、欲望，甚至突发的奇想。在十余年简约主义大肆盛行之后，人们将会重新面临一个强调重复和多样的审美时代。

本书谈到的新潮流，我们冒昧地称之为"极繁主义"，是各设计家们的艺术构想的集大成者，他们正在创造一种全新而复杂、具有折衷主义特性的现代作风。与一些正在迅速兴起的美学运动一起，"极繁主义"已经影响到各个学科领域，促进它们互相融合，创造出新的多学科综合性领域。以前卫著称的时尚设计就是"极繁主义"最先留下痕迹的领域之一。简朴的服装已经退出T型台，让位于以多种材料设计的时装，像杜尔斯·嘉巴纳、范思哲或维叶尼·维斯特伍德公司都在使用诸如皮革、漆皮、轻纱以及在衣料上缀得满满的装饰纽扣一类的材料。工业设计也在经历转变：那些造型简单、色调单一的家具所营造的舒适度已远远不能满足人们的需要。波浪型的书架、皮毛沙发、弯腿桌、动物形开罐器以及种种功能与想象相结合的新奇设计层出不穷。

"极繁主义"还影响到其他一些领域，比如珠宝、电影、文学和基于概念和技术工具的绘画设计，寻找凌驾于模糊、张力以及秩序之上的超越。在建筑业领域中也能察觉到类似的变化，有时还很夸张。建筑师们已摈弃了以往无处不见的混凝土及白色粉刷，开始使用新型建筑材料，如波纹金属板和玻璃嵌板。刻意的装饰不再是一种罪恶，织物、高级涂料以及结合了古典主义与未来派气息的家具使得空间更富色彩，这些空间仅有的同时也是最大的用途即是展现华美。

本书介绍了一批新的"极繁主义"建筑精品，众多建筑元素被层层叠加，反复使用，极尽华丽完美之能事。经精心挑选的公共建筑、写字楼和住宅"恭恭敬敬"地"触犯"了密斯·范德罗所谓的"少即是好"的座右铭，提出了"繁复永无停歇"的口号。

The artistic movements that have taken place throughout history have fluctuated periodically between exuberance and sobriety. This tendency to invert sophistication and simplicity can be observed in comparing movements as early as Roman and Gothic art: the first generated simple and purified forms impelled by a virtually nonexistent technique, while the second created more complicated geometries thanks to the advancement of constructive systems.

This tendency repeats itself once again in successive artistic movements, for example in the transformation of simple classical lines into the profusion of ornamental and baroque, which filled buildings with volutes, corbels, skirting boards, and cornices. In this way, upon entering the 20th century, the modern movement, whose aim was to simplify form and material, precedes postmodernism, in which the straight angle disappears and geometry becomes complex in order to offer a great variety of results. The cycle alternates once again in the early nineties with the birth of minimalism, a trend that intends to offer a break from the opulence of postmodernism and deconstructivism. This inclination to pursue simplicity turned into a fad; white, straight angles and subtlety as a design strategy were exploited to their very limits, saturating both creators and clients. A new system of artistic creation has appeared in response to this saturation, reflecting the necessity to produce a more complex art form. Through these projects, clients and designers intend to reproduce their needs, desires and whims. After more than ten years of the supremacy of minimalism, we live with expectancy the arrival of a new aesthetic that embraces variety and pluralism.

This new sensibility, which in this book we have ventured to call maximalism, gathers the objectives of designers who are constructing a new, complex and eclectic modernity. As with any aesthetic movement that starts off strongly, maximalism has affected all disciplines and has even prompted them to merge with each other, creating new multi-disciplinary projects. Fashion design, as avant-garde as always, was one of the first areas in which maximalism began leaving its mark. Austere clothes have disappeared from the catwalks and made room for garments that combine a variety of materials: leather, patent leather, gauze and studs impregnate the clothes of firms like Dolce & Gabbana, Versace or Vivienne Westwood. Industrial design is also experiencing a transformation: the comfort of furniture is no longer enough and originality is sought through singular forms and colors. Wave-shaped shelves, furry sofas, tables with curved legs, animal-shaped can-openers...and an endless variety of objects remarkable for their combination of functionality and imagination.

Maximalism has also transformed other practices such as jewelry, film, literature and graphic design based on conceptual and technical instruments that search for the transgression of ambiguities, tensions and orders. Architecture, however, is the practice in which these changes are most perceptible and in some case most exaggerated. Designers have left behind the omnipresent concrete, painted in white, and have begun to raise buildings with a fusion of new materials like corrugated metal sheeting or glass panels that change their transparency with the flip of a switch. The ornament is no longer a crime; fabrics, sophisticated finishings, and the mixture of antique and futuristic furniture comprise environments rich in sensations where the only yet sufficient utility is beauty.

This volume introduces a fresh batch of maximalist projects in which the superimposing of elements is carried out with a great deal of richness and perfection. The careful selection of public buildings, commercial and residential spaces humbly contradicts Mies°Ømaxim °∞less is more°±and establishes that more is never enough.

More is never enough

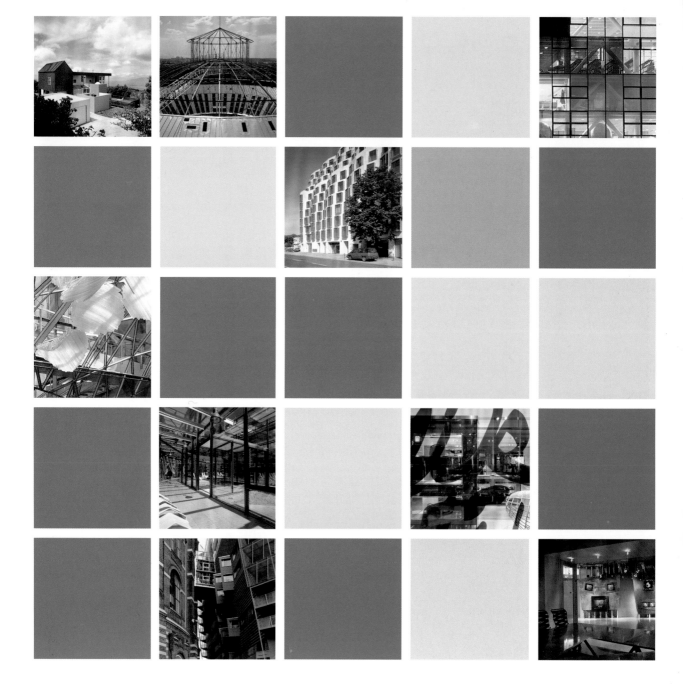

完 工 建 筑
FINISHED PROJECTS

扎哈·哈迪德建筑事务所 Zaha Hadid Architects

精神时空

精神时空是千禧年穹顶建筑群的14个独立展厅之一。位于伦敦以东泰晤士河畔一个半岛之上的千禧年穹顶，穹顶直径为365.7米，在它覆盖下的一大片场地都是以具有展览作用的"轮状物"及其圆形轨道为中心而组织的。14个主题展览区都被赋予"身体"、"游戏"、"工作"等有趣的名字。扎哈·哈迪德建筑所在工程竞标中胜出，负责建造称为精神时空的两个展区。

为完成这个工程，建筑师们建议将展览的主题和结构作为一个统一概念而同时考虑。完成这项工程就是一份使形式与功能完全结合的工作。建筑师们所面临的问题是如何不依赖其物理变形而表现意识。这项设计的基础是大脑与其所拥有的精神的复杂机理之间的分化，例如不断延伸、相互重叠的棚架就好像是大脑，它的外观设计源自对精神过程的抽象处理，旨在直接抓住参观者的眼球，并使参观者产生见仁见智的理解。该设计避免了过分浮夸，而是鼓励游客自己去体味和思考。

众多艺术家（包括理查德·迪肯和让·姆艾克）参加了合作，共同研究设计细节，在起伏的路线中为游人提供解释和启示。

THE PROJECT SOUGHT TO MATERIALIZE THE ABSTRACT REALM OF THE MIND, THOUGHTS AND CHEMICAL IMPULSES

这项工程寻求精神、思想和化学冲动的抽象范畴的物化。

The Mind Zone is one of the fourteen individual exhibition spaces in the Millennium Dome complex. Sited on a peninsula on the Thames River east of London, the Dome is a tensed circular fabric 1,200 ft. in diameter covering a large floor area organized around a central "wheel" for exhibits and a ring for circulation. The fourteen thematic exhibition areas were given names such as Body, Play, Work, and so on. The team led by Zaha Hadid won the competition to design two of these areas, called the Mind Zone.

For this commission, the architects proposed working simultaneously with the contents of the exhibition and its structure as a single concept. This approach to the project gave rise to a work in which form and function are totally integrated.

The problem posed was how to represent the mind without resorting to its physical manifestation. The project was developed on the basis of the differentiation between the brain and the complex mechanisms of the mind it houses, such that the pavilion-configured as a succession of continuous, overlapping areas would be the vital organ: its material presence refers to the abstraction of the mental processes, striking to the visitor's eye and inviting one to come to one's own conclusions. This design strategy eschewed excessive pedantry, instead seeking to encourage thought in the observer.

A number of artists (among them Richard Deacon and Ron Mueck) collaborated in the study of the design of the contents, which juxtapose evocation and explanation along an up-and-down route.

Mind Zone

展馆内部设计的独特之处就在于它和建造该展馆所使用的材料相融合：轻体、半透明的玻璃纤维嵌板位于城堡状铝制框架之上，覆盖在钢结构上，强化了空间的连续性。此外，它使得不同氛围空间可以进行视觉交流，同时也反映了展会为期仅一年的短暂特性。

最终，建筑师们创造出这样一个空间，拓展了仅能通过有形事物表现抽象的限制。

The singularity of the content was to have its correspondence in the materials employed in the construction of the container: fiberglass panels, lightweight and translucent, over a castellated aluminium framework, capping the steel structure and reinforcing the sensation of spatial continuity. In addition, this permitted visual communication between the different atmospheres and reflected the ephemeral character of an exhibition that was to last only a year.
The result was the creation of a space for exploring the limits at which the abstract could be attained only through the tangible.

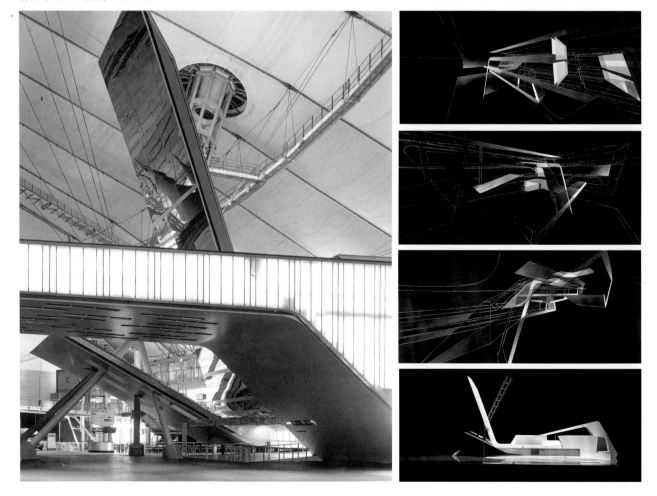

电脑模拟使扎哈·哈迪德的事务所可以处理工程中的抽象概念，这种方法有助于生成具联想性的外观，以表现大脑形成的抽象概念。这些模拟生成的主题也显示出该展馆在形式上建材交叠、功能交叉，颇具复杂性。

玻璃纤维嵌板可被切割成各种尺寸大小，方向也不受限制，因此可呈现多复杂几何图形，甚至曲线形式。材质半透明的特性使参观者可以围绕展馆参观，从外部也可看到内部的陈列。

Computer simulations allowed Zaha Hadid's studio to work with abstractions of the project, a strategy that would help generate evocative forms of the abstractions effected by the brain. These schemes also give an idea of the formal complexity of the result, where materials overlap and functions mix.
Fiberglass panels can be cut to size and in any direction, thus they can generate complex geometries and even curved shapes. Their translucence allows the movement of the users around the pavilion and the compositive elements inside to be seen from outside.

考虑到安全,立面的玻璃板包上了一层聚乙烯薄膜,当窗子破裂时可以避免碎片的飞溅。保护措施还可以确保空气的流通,但嵌板会出现一定的老化现象。

For safety reasons, the glass on the facades was laminated by applying a polyvinyl film, thus preventing broken windows from shattering. Moreover, this type of protection ensures proper ventilation, even though the panels may suffer some deterioration.

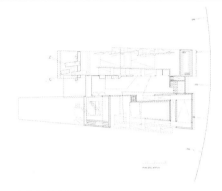

9 米高度平面图 FINISHED FLOOR LEVEL 30 FT.

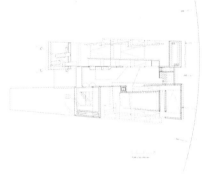

4.5 米高度平面图 FINISHED FLOOR LEVEL 15 FT.

0.6 米高度平面图 FINISHED FLOOR LEVEL 2 FT.

0 1 2

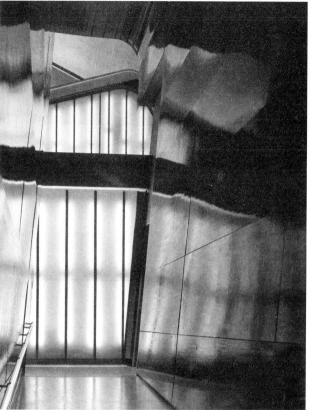

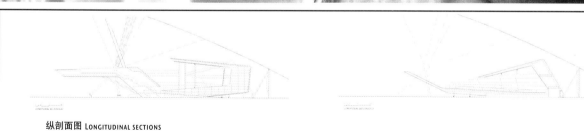

纵剖面图 LONGITUDINAL SECTIONS

建筑设计：扎哈·哈迪德建筑事务所
合作方：欧威·阿鲁珀事务所（建筑）、
　　　　荷兰照明公司（灯饰）
建造时间：1999 年
位置：英国 伦敦 千禧年穹顶
摄影：海伦·比奈特

ARCHITECTS: Zaha Hadid Architects
COLLABORATORS: Ove Arup & Partners (structures),
Hollands Licht (lighting).
BUILT: 1999
LOCATION: Millennium Dome, London, United Kingdom
PHOTOGRAPHY: Hélène Binet

贝尼施建筑事务所 Behnisch & Partner

巴德埃尔斯特温泉

巴德埃尔斯特温泉是德国最古老的泥炭沼温泉区之一。随着时光流逝，这座温泉经历了数次修缮，扩张并改善它的设施，反映出多种建筑风格。在竞标中胜出的贝尼施建筑事务所接手了重建建筑群体的挑战，重建工程包括拆除大量旧的建筑、建设一处新的温泉浴场和一所信息服务中心，以及重新安排现有空间。

原有的建筑都建在一座大的、方形庭院四周，面对着未经精心设计的建筑物后立面。颇有巴洛克风格的主立面突出而开敞，可以看得到城镇和附近的林地。设计师们的初衷是渐渐向建筑群灌输新的气象：重新设计中心区域，并试图使新建筑与现存的建筑达成和谐。

在这一设计中，以前用作仓库和预备泥浆用的庭院将成为整座建筑群体的中心，结构引人注目的新建浴场也是其中的一部分。新浴场的设计洋溢着极度的感性气息，被祥和与愉悦的气氛所环绕，再加上温泉的独特治疗功效，使这里成为一个理想的休闲胜地。

为加强温泉浴场内部与室外环境（森林和天空）的联系，避免形成庭院内的闭塞感，浴场的围护全部选用透明材料。

创新的建筑技术、深刻的生态意识是该浴场设计的指导方针。

THE DESIGN OF THE BATHHOUSE WAS GOVERNED BY INNOVATIVE CONSTRUCTION TECHNOLOGIES AND PROFOUND ECOLOGICAL AWARENESS

The Spa Bad Elster is one of the oldest peat moss spas in Germany. Through the years it has undergone numerous modifications to improve and enlarge its installations, and thus reflects diverse architectural styles. After winning the competition for the new work, the Behnisch & Partner studio faced the challenge of restructuring the complex, including the demolition of a number of obsolete buildings, the construction of a new bathhouse and an information center, as well as the rearrangement of the existing spaces. The original buildings are grouped around a large rectangular courtyard, on to which face in a somewhat helter-skelter manner the rear façades. The main façades, of which some in baroque style stand out, open outwards, with views of the town and the nearby woodlands. The architects' primary objective was to instill the complex with a new life: redesigning the central area and attempting to harmonize the new buildings with the existing ones.

With this project, the courtyard, formerly used as a storage area and to prepare the mud, became the heart of the complex, with the new bathhouse as its most outstanding structure. The design of the bathhouse was governed by extreme sensitivity: it was endowed with a peaceful and gratifying atmosphere which, along with its therapeutic virtues, make the building an ideal place to relax.

To strengthen the link between the interior of the bathhouse and the outdoor environment (woods and sky) and to avoid a hemmed-in feeling in the courtyard, transparent materials were chosen for all the enclosures. The façades and the roof consist of double-glazed glass, with a one-meter airspace between the layers. The exterior panels are

Spa Bad Elster

立面和屋顶均由双层玻璃构成，间距为1米，外侧的玻璃嵌板高度绝缘。玻璃嵌板之间装有高效通风系统，可以节约能源、防止凝水，在一年之中营造舒适的室内环境。此外，其间设置的一些小组件可将夹层中产生的热量用于冬季供暖。

屋顶系统内以彩色玻璃制成的百叶窗构成，可防止日晒和避免眩光。百叶窗的角度可以调节，夏天时调至适当位置便可提供阴凉。

highly insulating, while an efficient ventilation system was installed between the two layers to economize on energy, avoid condensation and create a comfortable indoor environment year round. In addition small units were installed to take advantage of the heat generated in the airspace to heat the complex in winter.

The construction system for the roof includes colored-glass louvers that offer protection from the sun and prevent glare. Since they are adjustable, in summer they can be set perpendicularly to provide shade.

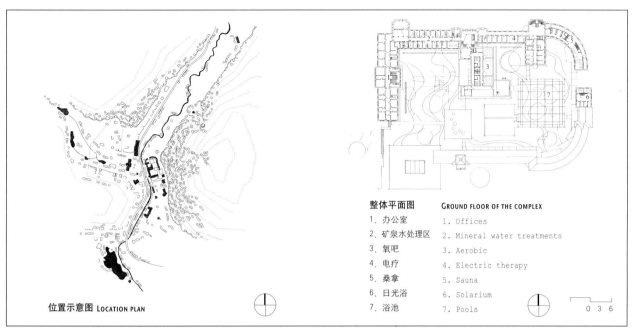

整体平面图 **GROUND FLOOR OF THE COMPLEX**

1、办公室　　　1. Offices
2、矿泉水处理区　2. Mineral water treatments
3、氧吧　　　　　3. Aerobic
4、电疗　　　　　4. Electric therapy
5、桑拿　　　　　5. Sauna
6、日光浴　　　　6. Solarium
7、浴池　　　　　7. Pools

位置示意图 LOCATION PLAN

0　3　6

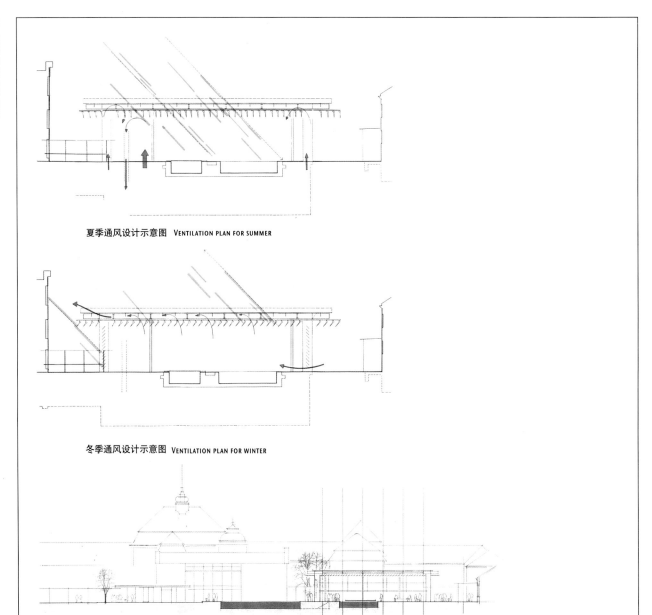

夏季通风设计示意图　VENTILATION PLAN FOR SUMMER

冬季通风设计示意图　VENTILATION PLAN FOR WINTER

纵向剖面图　LONGITUDINAL SECTION

0　1　2

建筑设计：贝尼施建筑事务所
合作方：卢兹事务所（景观设计）、
埃瑞克·维斯纳（色彩设计）
建造时间：1999 年
地点：德国 巴德埃尔斯特
总面积：17292 平方米
摄影：克里斯廷·坎德齐亚、马丁·斯科德

Architects: Behnisch & Partner
Collaborators: Luz & Partner (landscaping), Erich Wiesner (color study)
Built: 1999
Location: Bad Elster, Germany
Gross floor area: 186,236 sq. ft.
Photography: Christian Kandzia & Martin Schodder

盖瑞建筑事务所 Gehry Partners, LLP

DZ 银行

位于柏林市中心的DZ银行（德国中央银行）大厦是一座商住两用的综合型建筑，商业区包括了该银行在本市的重要办公室，正对着巴黎广场和著名的勃兰登堡门。住宅区包括39套公寓，面向相对安静的贝伦大街。

两个区域的立面皆以黄色石灰岩装饰，使这处新建筑的色彩可与现存的历史建筑相协调。大厦的外形比例也考虑到相邻的建筑，尝试着营造统一、和谐的城市氛围。巴黎广场一侧的立面最充分地体现了这一原则，窗户向后回缩，与附近的建筑保持一致。

一个巨大的玻璃屋顶遮蔽着银行大厦主入口。走过玻璃屋顶下方的通道，进入一个敞亮的前厅，这里可以见到这一设计的中心：一个气势庞大的中庭，上下都有拱状的玻璃结构。办公室被安排在中庭的周围，以获取更多的日照，一连串的包木拱廊将参观者引至中庭两侧的电梯。

楼内的主会议厅是一个位于中庭下方的玻璃拱结构之上的、具有雕塑感的空间，好像在空中飘浮。它的外部为不锈钢构成，内部则全部以木板镶嵌。

THE DZ BANK IS A PROJECT THAT COMBINES MASTERFULLY NUMEROUS DISCIPLINES, ARCHITECTURE, SCULPTURE AND PAINTING

DZ银行工程巧妙地将建筑艺术、雕刻和绘画等领域结合在一起。

The DZ Bank building, located in the heart of Berlin, is a hybrid complex that accommodates residential and commercial uses. The commercial part houses the bank's main offices in the city and faces the Pariser Platz and the historic Brandenburg Gate. The residential area, comprising 39 flats, looks on to a quieter street, Behrenstrasse. Both façades were erected with yellow limestone so that the color of the new construction would match the existing historic buildings. The composition of the enclosures was also adapted to the proportions of the neighboring buildings, in an attempt to create a singular, coherent urban environment. A good example of this strategy is the Pariser Platz façade, where the windows were set back in keeping with the adjacent buildings.

A large glass roof shelters the main entrance to the bank building. One passes under the glass hood and enters an enormous lobby from which one sees the centerpiece of the project: a spectacular interior atrium crowned with a vaulted roof, made of glass, as is the floor. The offices are arrayed around this grand courtyard to take advantage of the luminosity it offers. A series of wood-clad arcades lead to the elevators, located at either side of the atrium. The main conference hall of the complex is located in a sculptured volume over the glass floor of the atrium, giving it the appearance of floating in space. The exterior of the body is of stainless steel and the interior is entirely panelled in wood, thus creating a warm and comfortable atmosphere for meetings. Other common rooms are in the basement arrayed around a large hall, where the café is

DZ Bank

为会议大厅营造出舒适温馨的气氛。一层的公共休息室环列在附有咖啡厅的大厅四周。举办大型会议或宴会时，可将这些空间并入大厅。住宅区同样以庭院为中心，这里的庭院不太大，但是仍然可为公寓提供两侧的自然日照。一层内小型水池闪烁出的粼粼波光，在玻璃的过廊和电梯之中都可看到。

大厦公寓的类型各不相同，其中既有小型工作室，也有豪华的顶层复式观景公寓。

also located. These spaces can be joined to accommodate large conventions or banquets.

The residential area is also centerd on a courtyard, which, though smaller, still affords the flats natural light on two sides. The water in a small pool on the ground floor produces numerous luminous effects, reflections and iridescences which can be seen from the glass corridors and elevators.

A range of residences was designed for the building, from small studios to a pair of luxurious top-floor duplexes with magnificent views of the city.

这张图清晰地显示出庭院屋架系统的复杂结构，这些几何线条是在电脑软件以及建筑模型的帮助下完成的，弗兰克·O.盖瑞所领导的工作室经常使用这些方法。

The sections show clearly the formal complexity of the roof system of the courtyards. These geometries are generated with the aid of computer programes and the building of models, a method used profusely at the studio headed by Frank O. Gehry.

总平面图 LOCATION PLAN

　　住宅区立面俯瞰着一条安静的大街,起伏的外观形成单一特性。立面上所有阳台朝向不同角度,形成复杂的立面构图。高层部分向后回缩,形成小型露台。

　　住宅的阳台由铝合金架制成,玻璃围栏被铆焊于钢铁构件上。突出立面表面的部分以玻璃在前方和两侧加以围合。

The façade of the residences, overlooking a quiet street, acquires a singular character from the undulation of the facing. All the balconies, moreover, project at different angles from the plane, thus attaining a complex composition. The upper floors are set back to create small terraces. The balconies of the residences are made of an aluminum skeleton and a glass railing riveted to the metal work. The volume projecting from the façade is enclosed in glass at the front and sides.

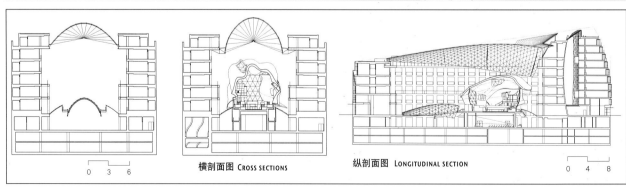

横剖面图 CROSS SECTIONS

0 3 6

纵剖面图 LONGITUDINAL SECTION

0 4 8

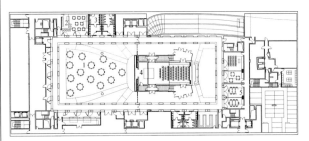

地下一层 BASEMENT

1．咖啡厅
2．酒吧
3．卫生间
4．礼堂
5．会议厅

1. Café
2. Bar
3. Toilets
4. Auditorium
5. Conference hall

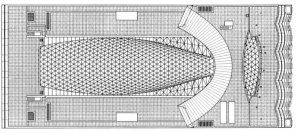

底层平面图 GROUND FLOOR

1．阳台庭院
2．会议厅
3．办公室
4．电梯

1. Patio
2. Conference Hall
3. Offices
4. Elevator

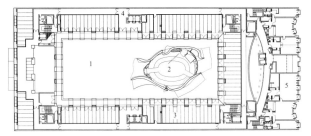

二层平面图 FIRST FLOOR

1．庭院
2．会议厅
3．办公室
4．电梯
5．住宅

1. Courtyard
2. Conference hall
3. Offices
4. Elevators
5. Residences

屋顶平面图 ROOF PLAN

0　1　2

建筑设计：盖瑞建筑事务所
合作方：穆勒·马尔工程公司和施莱
赫·博格曼事务所（建筑结构）、布兰
迪工程公司（机械与电气）
建造时间：2001 年
地址：德国 柏林
总面积：17689 平方米
摄影：罗兰·哈尔比

Architects: Gehry Partners, LLP
Collaborators: Ingenieur Büro
Müller Marl GmbH and Schlaich
Bergermann und Partner
(structures), Brandi Ingenieure
GmbH (mechanical/electrical)
Built: 2001
Location: Berlin, Germany
Gross floor area: 215,053 sq. ft
Photography: Roland Halbe

卡普斯建筑事务所 Caps Architects

克里斯汀－拉克鲁瓦服装店

　　克里斯托弗·卡朋特领导的瑞士卡普斯建筑事务所，受雇设计位于东京的新克里斯汀·拉克鲁瓦服装店。店主拉克鲁瓦过去曾与该事务所合作过几次，他提出了一定的设计预想："工程必须基于即定的环境开展，它要体现建筑室的意愿，但不能置现有建筑框架于不顾。"从工程的初期开始，卡朋特就希望将此项工程设计成一个吸引旅客流连观光的场所，富于变化，每一块空间都能迎合人们的特殊需要。

　　商店分上下两层，四周环以通透的玻璃立面，上面套印了拉克鲁瓦漂亮的手写体。两个楼层之间的楼板不与立面相交，以一条细微的铝合金框架分割，从而使立面具有连绵不绝的感觉。

　　两个楼层的布局都是由商品陈列位置决定的。装饰物和陈设品引导着顾客的购物线路，装饰物和陈设可以移动，使商店布局很容易产生变化。陈设架由彩色透明玻璃组件构成，带给公众顾客幻彩般的视觉感受。由设计师皮埃尔·保林设计的曲线型椅子、以柔软的金色天鹅绒织物勾勒出有机外型的试衣间，与这些陈设架的直角形成鲜明对照。

"我们希望超越简单的白色立方空间设计，寻求重新建立几何图形与有机物质之间的平衡。"

The Swiss studio Caps Architects, led by Christophe Carpente, was commissioned to design the new Christian Lacroix clothing shop in Tokyo. Lacroix, who had already worked with the architects on previous occasions, set out certain premises: "The project must respect the chosen setting; despite a forceful implantation of the firm's presence, the shop cannot ignore the architectural framework into which it is being introduced." From the outset Carpente sought a project which oozes temporality, which evokes the nomadism of travellers, capable of change, of adapting itself to the specific needs of each space.

The shop is distributed on two floors and enclosed within a totally transparent façade overprinted with a calligraphy text by Lacroix himself. The between-floors slab does not meet the façade, thus the enclosure appears continuous, broken up only by a subtle aluminium-work framing.

The layout of both floors is governed by the deployment of the displays. The customer's itinerary is marked out by these furnishings, which are moveable to make the shop easily transformable. The displays were conceived as transparent coloured-glass modules offering the public varied perspectives of different hues. The right angles of these furnishings contrast with the curvy chairs by the designer Pierre Paulin, as well as with the fitting rooms, shells of organic contours lined with silky, golden velvety fabrics. The existing structure of the premises remained unchanged and only the distribution was altered, tearing out all the partitions while the preserved outer walls were painted completely white with a subtle coat of nacre. These sur-

"WE WANTED TO GO BEYOND SIMPLE WHITE CUBES TO RE-ESTABLISH THE BALANCE BETWEEN GEOMETRY AND ORGANICS"

Boutique Christian Lacroix

现有的房屋结构保持不变，只是在布局方面进行一些改动，拆除所有隔离墙，留下的外墙全部涂成精细的珍珠白。墙面挂满了艺术家以及公司合作者的照片，如乔尔·巴托罗米欧、戴尔芬尼·克鲁特、尼尔斯·尤多和伯纳德·奎斯尼奥。电气装置隐藏在金属箱内，使人联想起孩童经常玩耍的积木。灯光设备系统则是由直接指向服装和彩色陈列架的聚光灯组成。

faces serve for the projection of videos and photos by artists and some of the firm's habitual collaborators, such as Joël Bartolomeo, Delphine Kreuter, Nils Udo and Bernard Quesniaux. The electrical fittings were concealed in stacked metal boxes which recall those old building blocks kids used to play with. The lighting consists of spotlamps directed at the clothing and coloured furnishings.

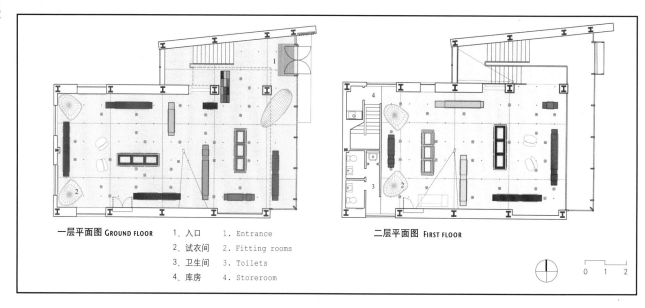

一层平面图 GROUND FLOOR

1、入口　　1. Entrance
2、试衣间　2. Fitting rooms
3、卫生间　3. Toilets
4、库房　　4. Storeroom

二层平面图 FIRST FLOOR

0　1　2

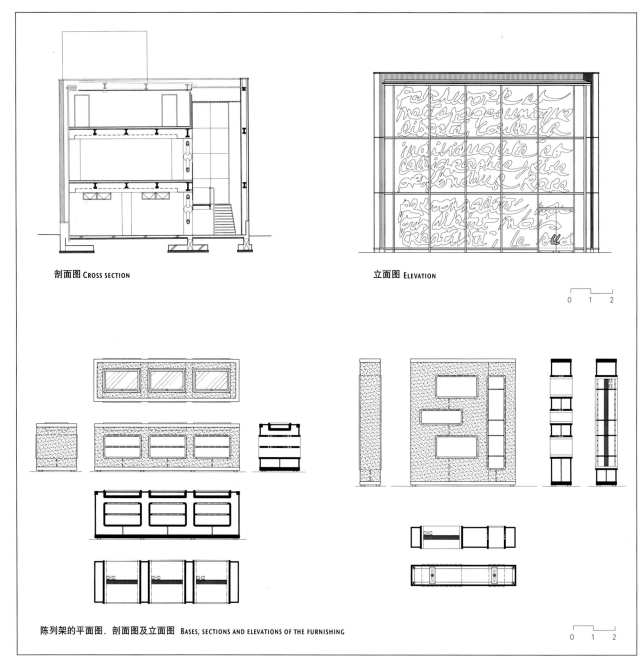

剖面图 Cross section

立面图 Elevation

0 1 2

陈列架的平面图、剖面图及立面图 Bases, sections and elevations of the furnishing

0 1 2

建筑设计：卡普斯建筑事务所
合作方：尤诺·格拉斯公司（家具制造）、大林组建
筑公司（建筑）、艾克斯设计公司（当地建筑师）、安
索格公司（照明）、格雷斯公司（全息摄影胶片）
建造时间：2001年
地址：日本 东京
总面积：250平方米
摄影：纳卡萨事务所

Architect: Caps Architects
Collaborators: Ueno Glass (furniture
production), Obayashi Construction
(building), Axe design (local architects),
Ansorg GmbH (light), Glace Controle
(holographics films)
Built: 2001
Location: Tokyo, Japan
Gross floor area: 2,688 sq. ft
Photography: Nácasa & Partners

阿尔索普和斯托默尔建筑事务所 Alsop & Stormer

佩克汉姆图书馆

佩克汉姆图书馆是伦敦东南佩克汉姆地区城市改造项目的一部分。它与1998年建造的现代体育中心和整修的城市设施一起，也成为了该地区的一道新景观。

地方当局提出了非常明确的要求：超前的设计可使周边区域远近闻名，同时又要避免独特的造型给使用者带来不适，公众应对它表示认同。设计的另一目的是创造一个方便灵活的公共场馆，足以满足未来几代人的需求。

建筑家阿尔索普和斯托默尔设计的图书馆，呈倒立的英文大写字母"L"形，一块高出街面12米、水平方向的砌块，由几根圆柱和垂直方向的砌块共同支撑。这项设计为户外活动设计了有遮蔽的场地。除此之外，悬挑部分遮挡了南面外墙，因此不必增设窗帘或其他遮阳物。屋顶高达2米的巨大不锈钢字母标识使图书馆的外观更显独特。

水平方向的砌块内含一个两层空间，设立了服务台、阅览区，北部是儿童图书馆。由圆柱支撑的3个大型卵形空间，分别设为非洲－加勒比文学中心、儿童活动区和会议大厅。最大的空间被一块橙色的天窗式屋架所覆盖，远远地从街道上就可一目了然。

THE LIBRARY IS PART OF AN URBAN REGENERATION PROGRAM FOR THE PECKHAM AREA

这座图书馆是佩克汉姆区城市改造项目的一部分。

This project is part of a major urban renewal program for the Peckham area in southeast London. In conjunction with other projects, such as the construction of a modern sports center in 1998 or the refurbishing of the urban furnishings, the library creates a new landscape.

The local authorities who commissioned the work were very clear about their requirements: the building was to bring prestige to the neighborhood with a design that was ahead of its time while eschewing an elitist appearance that might inhibit users: the public should be able to identify with the building. The goal was also to create a flexible facility, adaptable to the needs of future generations.

The library designed by the architects Alsop & Stormer takes the shape of an inverted "L", with a horizontal block raised twelve meters above street level and supported partially on columns and partially on a vertical block. This design creates a covered space for outdoor activities. In addition, the cantilevered volume shades the south façade, such that neither blinds nor any other sort of sun protection were needed. Enormous stainless-steel lettering two meters tall contributes to the building's peculiar silhouette. The horizontal block consists of a double-height space that houses the main desk, the book area and, at the north, the children's library. Three ovoid volumes on columns that house a center for Afro-Caribbean literature, a children's activities area and a conference hall inhabit this large area. Capping the largest space is a large orange skylight-roof that can be seen from the street.

The main façade is covered by metal mesh, while the south, east and west enclosures are clad in copper panels. The

Peckham Library

图书馆的正立面覆有一层金属丝网，它的东、南、西向立面的外墙都贴以铜制嵌板。垂直部分的窗户采用彩色玻璃，用硅树脂固定于铝制合金窗框之上，构成一道奇特的幕墙。

图书馆的设计充分利用了自然能源，将燃料的消耗降至最低。由于设计者在环保方面作了明智周详的考虑，使得该工程在采光和通风方面获益良多，成为一幢真正符合生态要求的建筑。

windows of the vertical block are of colored glass fixed with silicone to aluminium frames, forming a peculiar curtain wall.

The library was designed to take advantage of natural energy sources and thus minimize fuel consumption. Thanks to wise environmental advisement, the project gets the most out of sunlight and ventilation, making it a truly ecological building.

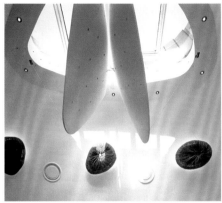

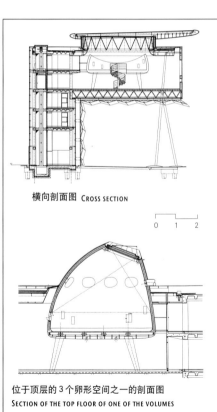

横向剖面图 CROSS SECTION

0　1　2

位于顶层的 3 个卵形空间之一的剖面图
SECTION OF THE TOP FLOOR OF ONE OF THE VOLUMES

0　0.5　2

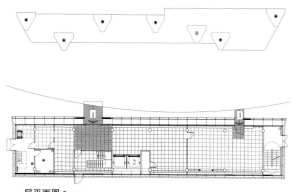

一层平面图 Ground floor

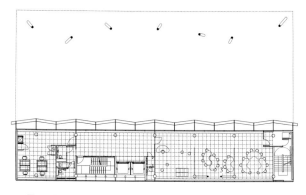

三层平面图 Second floor

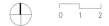

0　1　2

1、入口	1. Entrance
2、电梯	2. Elevators
3、会议厅	3. Conference hall
4、书籍图书区	4. Books
5、阅览室	5. Reading room
6、非洲-加勒比文学中心	6. Afro-Caribbean literature section
7、儿童图书馆	7. Children's library

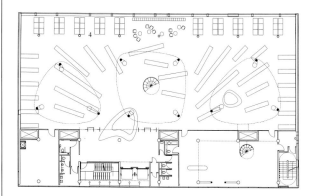

五层平面图 Fourth floor

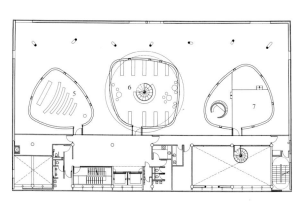

六层平面图 Fifth floor

这些卵形空间看上去好像3个入侵的天外来客。它们与建筑的交叉点非常巧妙，在天花板上形成一些天窗。它们的外部包以胶合板，内墙涂有灰泥。

The three volumes seem to invade the space, like alien objects. The intersection with the structure of the building is quite skilful and at the ceiling generates several skylights. These bodies are clad in aircraft ply, while the interior walls are finished in plaster.

建筑设计：阿尔索普和斯托默尔建筑事务所
合作方：亚当斯·卡拉·泰勒（建筑结构）、
协和照明设计公司（照明）、巴特尔·麦卡西
（环境工程）
建造时间：1999 年
地址：英国 伦敦
摄影：罗德里奇·考尼

ARCHITECTS: Alsop & Stormer
COLLABORATORS: Adams Kara Taylor (structures), Concord Lighting Design (lighting), Battle McCarthy (environmental engineering)
BUILT: 1999
LOCATION: London, United Kingdom
PHOTOGRAPHY: Roderick Coyne

菲尔德曼和基廷联合事务所 Felderman & Keatinge Associates

MTV 电视网总部

在着手设计工作之前，建筑师菲尔德曼和基廷就把目标锁定了位于美国西海岸的MTV新总部。这一工程的设计目标是：建造一个实用、温馨的办公空间，五层楼中的每一层都要体现迥然不同的美学观点。这座建筑既要与整个城市环境相融，又要能成为该公司的象征，展现公司的独特理念。为了满足这些要求，设计师们提出了一个创造性的建筑方案，充分体现出该公司在娱乐业和通讯业的领导地位。

建筑师最初将精力投注在如何建立一个能将建筑物与大海及当地植被紧密联系的入口。通过一个铺有沙滩般色彩的地面的小广场，就可进入大厅，这使人们不由联想起当地内外分界非常模糊的传统建筑。大楼三层、五层的立面以金属嵌板装饰，使人联想起大海中起伏的波浪。一个巨大的船形标志上，以粗犷的钢制字母宣示着公司的名称。

参观者走进大厅，迎面而来的是一辆漂亮的、1957年生产的流线型拖车，它被用做等候室。拖车内部有粉红色地毯、黑白花色的亚麻油毡以及塑料贴面的桌子，再现出20世纪50年代的风情。

THE WORK ENCOMPASSES A RANGE OF FINISHES, FURNITURE OF DIFFERENT VINTAGES AND EXPOSED FITTINGS, CREATING A VERY HETEROGENEOUS WHOLE

该设计包括一系列不同年代的家具以及外露装置，营造了一个光怪陆离的统一整体。

Before embarking on the design work, the architects Felderman & Keatinge set out the goals for the new MTV Networks headquarters on the west coast of the United States. The brief required functional and comfortable, almost homelike, work spaces, distributed on five floors, each endowed with distinct aesthetics. In addition, the building had to blend in with and respect the urban environment as well as stand out as a symbol of the company, establishing a unique corporate identity capable of representing the company's philosophy. In response to all these requirements, the designers came up with an innovative architecture that reflected the client's reputation as a leader in the entertainment and communications industry.

The first efforts were invested in creating an entrance that would link the building with the sea and local vegetation. A plaza with sand-colored flooring leads into the lobby, recalling the entries of the area's traditional architecture where the dividing line between outside and inside is blurred. The façade consists of three- and five-storey metal panels forming a profile that evokes the ocean waves. An enormous boat-shaped sign announces the name of the company in rough-hewn steel lettering.

A stunning 1957 Airstream aluminium trailer greets visitors and serves as a waiting room. Inside, the decoration recreates the fifties: a pink carpet, white and black linoleum and a formica-topped kitchen table. Next to the trailer television monitors are deployed in the shape of a face, giving the sensation that the images beam out of the eyes and mouth. The lobby is also furnished with a reception

MTV Networks Headquarters

拖车旁边的监视器被布置成人脸的形状，给人们造成这样一种感觉：电视画面仿佛是从眼睛和嘴里突现出来的。大厅内摆放着一张外包铝合金、船架状的接待桌以及一张铜贴面的会议桌。办公区由低矮的、房屋立面般的隔板隔开，上面带有铰链门式窗、木制壁板、花园栅栏、树篱和树木。根据客户对空间设计的非正式化要求，会议室按照起居室的风格设计，设有电视机、地毯和沙发。

desk made of a boat skeleton clad in aluminium and a copper-topped conference table.

The offices are separated by low partitions made to look like the house façades, including casement windows, wood siding, garden fences and painted-on hedges and trees. In keeping with the client's requirement that the spaces should be informal, the conference rooms were designed in living-room style, with televisions, carpets and sofas.

大楼内部采用朴素的水泥墙面, 以彩色的绘木、羊毛编织品、薄纱和金属板镶嵌。这一类的装饰从其他典型的办公室细部装饰中也同样可以见到。

The interior combines an austere concrete skeleton covered with sophisticated finishes and materials such as painted wood, braided wool fabrics, gauze curtains and metal panels. Glimpses of the fittings and structure can be seen among all the typical office elements and decorative details.

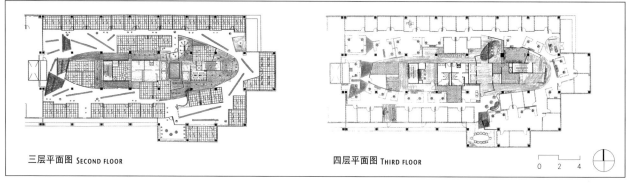

三层平面图 SECOND FLOOR

四层平面图 THIRD FLOOR

0 2 4

建筑设计：菲尔德曼和基廷联合事务所
建造时间：1999 年
地址：美国 圣莫尼卡
总建筑面积：10218 平方米
摄影：出山吉见

Architects: Felderman & Keatinge Associates
Built: 1999
Location: Santa Monica, United States
Gross floor area: 110,000 sq. ft.
Photography: Toshi Yoshimi

蓝天组事务所 Coop Himmelb(l)au

B 煤气厂

由 4 个煤气罐组成的一套老旧的煤气贮存设备曾负责整个维也纳的煤气供应。煤气厂关闭之后，旧设备被拆毁，只剩下残留的砖墙。由于该建筑物群在工业区的特殊位置以及该空间不同寻常的特色，多年来它们一直被当作文化中心，举办了许多种活动。

如果这次翻新工程伴随着交通系统的改善一同进行，包括修建一条地下铁路和新的高速公路，那么由煤气厂的地理位置决定，这将是扩展这座位于维也纳近郊的建筑物的一个绝好机会。除蓝天组以外，还有其他 3 家建筑工作室也参加了此项工程，具体工作包括：提出新建部分的设计理念；设计一座购物中心和一处综合娱乐场所，从而使这里变成维也纳一个新的焦点。

蓝天组负责扩展 B 煤气厂的计划，承担 3 个新增附属部分的建设：煤气厂内一座巨大的圆柱体建筑、位于圆柱体前侧的盾形公寓和基部可举办各种活动的多功能空间。

公寓和办公室位于新的圆柱形建筑内部，设计中还包含一个圆锥形的庭院，以便使圆柱体建筑内部获得充足的光线，而北向的阳台也为公寓的采光起到同样作用。大楼内共有 360 套公寓，其中既有附带阳台的家居住宅，也有为学生准备的小型工作间。这种将办公和居住宅功能相互结合的设计是为了尝试在单一环境中营造出生活、工作的新方式。

THE GASOMETERS CONSTITUTE THE FOCUS
OF A NEW URBAN CENTER IN VIENNA

煤气厂成为维也纳新的城区中心的焦点

The four Gasometers comprise an old gas storage facility that once supplied Vienna. After being closed down the facility was demolished, with only the striking brick façades left standing. The particular location of these buildings in an industrial area, along with the unusual character of the resulting spaces, led to their being used for years as cultural centers for numerous activities.

The location of the project presented a magnificent opportunity to develop the urban fabric on the outskirts of Vienna, given that the renovation went hand-in-hand with improvements in the transport system, including the extension of a metro line and the construction of a new motorway. Apart from Coop Himmelb(l)au, three other architecture studios participated in the project, designing new housing concepts, a shopping center and a leisure complex, converting the site into a new focal point for the city.

The project developed by Coop Himmelb(l)au for Gasometer B entailed the addition of three new volumes: a large cylinder inside the Gasometer, a striking shield-shaped flat block just beside the latter, and a multifunctional space for holding different sorts of events at the base.

Flats and offices were located inside the cylinder and in the new building. A conical courtyard was designed to provide natural light for the indoor spaces of the cylinder, while north-facing balconies serve the same function for the flats in the new building. The 360 residences range in type from spacious homes with terraces to small studios for students. The combination of office and residential uses is intended to generate new ways of living and working in a single environment.

Gasometer B

从大街或地铁站都可以直接进入煤气厂，但来访者和居民各有不同的入口。原来4个煤气厂内部通过购物中心相连接，并由此增加了综合建筑物基部的所在区域的长度。

公寓群的主体是由一系列从地面直达屋顶的混凝土立柱组成的系统。公寓外部由玻璃和铝制合金幕墙所包围，它们有限的厚度，使公寓内部能够获得更多的阳光。

独特的设计、新公寓的落成、购物、休闲和文化新区的创建、整个工业区的重建这种种举措，使得煤气厂成为维也纳新的城市中心。

Access to the Gasometer, with different entrances for visitors and residents, is from the street or directly from the metro station. All the former Gasometers are interconnected through the shopping center, which stretches the length of the base of the complex.

The structure of the flat block is comprised of a system of concrete columns rising from foundation to roof. Glass and aluminum curtain walls enclose the flats, which thanks to their limited depth get plenty of sunlight.

The extraordinariness of the project, the provision of new residences, the creation of a shopping, leisure and cultural area, and the regeneration of this industrial district have made the Gasometers Vienna's alternative urban center.

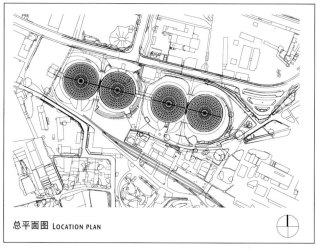

总平面图 LOCATION PLAN

这项工程由于蓝天组事务所采用了精湛的技术而闻名，他们借助这些技术解决了重建原有煤气贮存设施的问题，对新建建筑进行了大胆设计并创造性地改变了建筑物的外观。这是一项令人注目的工程，是过去与未来的合二为一。

The project developed by Coop Himmelb(l)au is notable for the skill with which they resolved the restoration of the former gas storage facility, with the forthrightness of the design of the new building, with its markedly innovative shapes. The complex is a prodigious fusion of past and future.

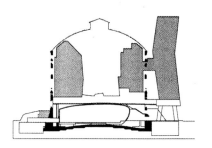

公寓 Flats

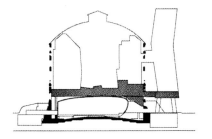

购物中心 Shopping Mall

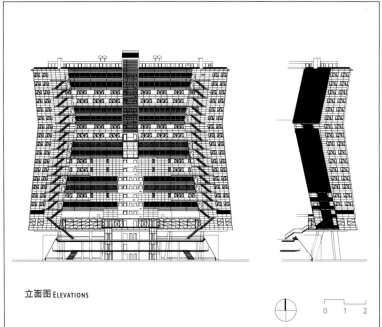

立面图 Elevations

0 1 2

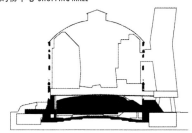

休闲区 Leisure

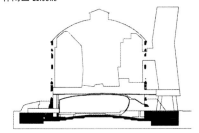

功能分区·停车场 Functional scheme. Parking

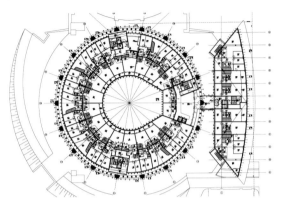

第 11 层平面图 Tenth floor

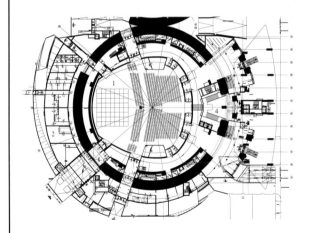

地下室平面图 Basement

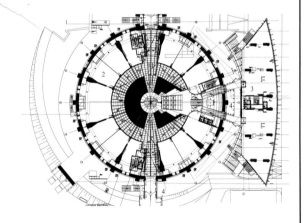

一层平面图 Ground floor

1、礼堂	1.Auditorium
2、办公室	2. Offices
3、住宅区	3. Housing
4、入口	4. Entrance
5、庭院	5. Courtyard

鉴于工程的规模，设计组需要绘制各种各样内部空间的草案图。住宅、办公室、购物中心、通道和通讯设施以及交流空间都按通常的设计要求进行设计，如：考虑生态环境、自然资源的充分利用，从而将这里转化为一个温馨、舒适的环境。

The scale of the project required the sketching of an enormous diversity of interior spaces. Housing, offices, shopping centers, and spaces for access and communication were designed with common objectives: ecology and maximum use of natural resources, translating into warmth and comfort.

建筑设计：蓝天组事务所
合作方：弗里特什－次埃里公司（结构建设），
克里斯－亚当斯公司（照明）
建造时间：2000 年
地址：奥地利 维也纳
总面积：23673 平方米
摄影：吉拉尔德·祖格曼

Architects: Coop Himmelb(l)au
Collaborators: Fritsch-Chiari (structures), Kress & Adams (lighting)
Built: 2000
Location: Vienna, Austria
Gross floor area: 376,344 sq. ft.
Photography: Gerald Zugmann

兰·威尔逊建筑文化事务所
Lang Wilson Practice in Architecture Culture

建筑学院

扩建建筑学院是基于智利圣玛利亚科技大学的要求开展的。首先，必须对扩建工程的功能和空间作出设计。从设计绘图到学院开学只有10个月时间，其中3个月用来设计，1个月计算费用，6个月开展建设工程。然而，更大的限制是在极少的预算条件下修建一栋面积为1792平方米的大楼。最后，扩建工程与原有建筑的关系将成为设计的重点，同时考虑结构（这里是地震多发区）以及风格上的要求（院内现有建筑全是新哥特式建筑，已被联合国编入目录）。

在通过设计满足以上要求之后，建筑师的关注点就是创造一个易于变化的空间，以应对建筑学院经常遇到的一些不可预知的设计变化。它既要实现建筑功能，同时又要方便未来的改造，因此建筑师提议建造一个在某种程度上来说不曾完成的建筑。它不受特定功能的限制，是一个可以开展各种活动的基础空间。

最前沿的电脑设计对于建造这样一个拥有多种用途的空间居功至伟。最后的设计结果远远超越了传统的公共建筑类型。

第一步的工作，是要建起一个通向多功能大空间的坡道，这个大空间既可以作为展览馆、机房、活动大厅，也可以仅作为一个散步的场所。第二步工作，则是要在原建筑物的顶部增加一个可容纳250人的室外礼堂。

THE RELATIONSHIP BETWEEN THE EXISTING BUILDINGS AND THE NEW EXPANSION IS INTERESTING IN ITS INGENIOUS USE OF CONTRASTS

设计者巧妙地运用了对比手法，使现有建筑物与扩建部分形成一种极为有趣的联系。

The commission was based on the requirements of the Universidad Técnica Federico Santa María for the expansion of the architecture school. In the first place, the project had to redefine the functional and spatial design of the expansion of the existing building. Moreover, a period of only ten months was allowed from the initial sketches to the opening of the school, leaving three months for the design, one for calculating costs and awarding the building work, and six for the actual construction. A further restriction was the limited budget for a 19,300 sq. ft. building. Finally, emphasis was placed on the relationship with the existing buildings, both at the structural level-given that this is an area of high seismic risk and at the formal level, by which the result would have to respect the other buildings on the campus, all in neo-gothic style and catalogued by the United Nations.

Once the requirements had been met, the architects' primary objective was to create a flexible space capable of evolving with the unpredictable design changes to which architecture schools are subject. To accommodate variable functions and future renovations, they proposed a building to a certain extent unfinished: a space which acts as an infrastructure for varied events rather than as a volume for fixed activities.

The use of cutting-edge computer design aided enormously in generating a space capable of accommodating a variety of uses. The virtual sequences served to move beyond the classic institutional typologies.

In the first stage of the work a ramp was erected leading to a large multifunctional space that can serve as an exhibition gallery, as a computer room, as an events hall or simply as an area for walking about. The second stage will add an exterior auditorium for 250 people on the roof.

Architecture School

材料的选择考虑到两方面因素，既要保护环境，又要尽可能创造出丰富多彩的视觉效果。设计师通过穿孔波纹状铝合金板材、玻璃幕墙和半透明防碎聚碳酸脂嵌板的运用使扩建部分与现有建筑融合得更好。这种立面还便于控制进入室内的光线，在酷暑时将进光量降至最低，同时半悬空的坡道还可以为原有建筑的遮蔽阳光。

The choice of materials was governed by environmental awareness and by the intention to create varied visual effects. The integration of this work with the existing buildings is achieved through the use of wavy perforated aluminum, a glass curtain wall and translucent polycarbonate panels. In addition, the façade system permits control of the light entering the interior and minimizes the transmission of heat during the hot summer months. Meanwhile, the suspended ramp acts as a blind.

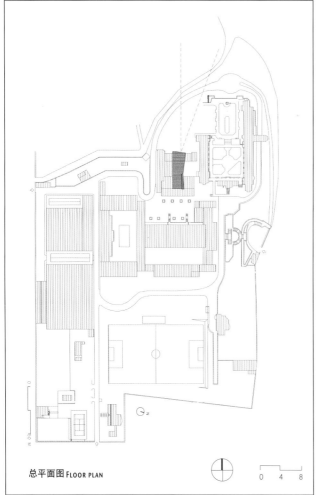

总平面图 FLOOR PLAN

0 4 8

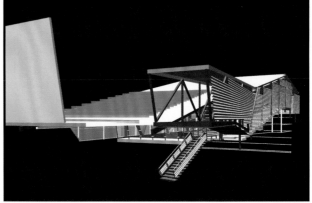

屋顶新建的桁架结构在其内部有非常鲜明的体现。地板铺设在倾斜的圆柱上，这些承重元素也因而显得更为突出。

The trussed structural system for the roof stands out boldly in the interior. The flooring reflects the inclined columns, emphasizing the presence of the load-bearing elements.

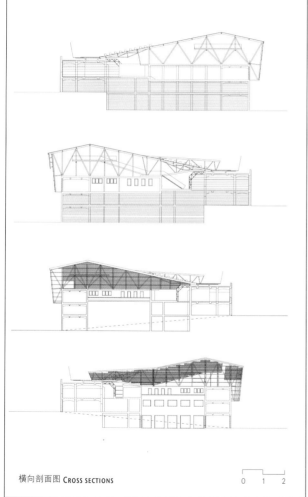

横向剖面图 CROSS SECTIONS

0 1 2

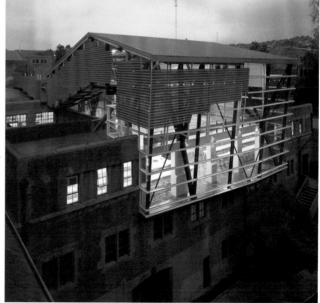

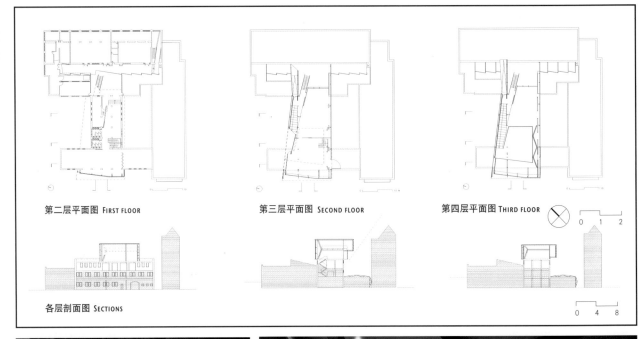

第二层平面图 First floor   第三层平面图 Second floor   第四层平面图 Third floor

0 1 2

各层剖面图 Sections

0 4 8

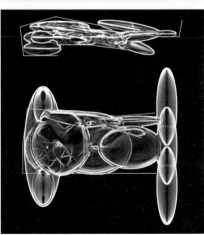

建筑设计：兰·威尔逊建筑文化事务所
合作方：罗伯托·巴利亚、保尔·泰勒、利卡多·卢纳公司（建筑结构）、麦诺斯公司（承包商）、奥斯卡·瑞利尔（技术监督）
建造时间：1999 年
地址：智利 瓦尔帕莱索
总面积：1792 平方米
摄影：居伊·温波尼

Architects: LWPAC, Lang Wilson Practice in Architecture Culture
Collaborators: Roberto Barria, Pol Taylor, Ricardo Luna SA (structures), Mainos SA (contractor) and Oscar Jalil (technical supervisor).
Built: 1999
Location: Valparaiso, Chile
Gross floor area: 19,300 sq. ft.
Photography: Guy Wenborne

埃托里·索特萨斯 Ettore Sottsass

奥拉布薇娜格别墅

意大利建筑师埃托里·索特萨斯设计了这座以毛伊岛光影为背景的专有别墅，现为阿克米工作室所有。它位于一座小山之上，俯瞰着浩瀚的海景。

两根同色、伸入地下的细柱，以及它们支撑的黑色板型屋顶构成了该建筑的构架。在这个状似大桌的屋顶下，几个材料和颜色各不相同的独立形体组合在一起。索特萨斯总是偏重于运用色彩创造奇异的建筑世界，而这所建筑就是其中一个典型样例。

别墅入口处设有一扇直通室内的红色拱门，室内平和的风格与建筑独特的立面形成鲜明的对照。建筑一层是公共空间，设有起居室、餐室厅、厨房和书房，所有房间都铺着美国的橡木地板。起居室的四壁都装有大尺寸的玻璃嵌板，满足了光线及视野两方面的需要。

所有的窗子都没有配备窗帘，以免将内外环境完全隔开。不过，为了防止眩光的产生，组成这座建筑的各个形体被设计成不同的高度和尺寸，确保所有房间都有遮挡，比如起居室就处于卧室所处的形体形成的阴凉之中。

场地斜坡的问题是这样解决的：修建一个巨大的平台，再把房子建在平台之上。

The Italian architect Ettore Sottsass designed this single-family residence, currently owned by the Acme Studios company, using as a reference the light and the shadows of the island of Maui, where it is located. The house was built atop a hill with magnificent views of the sea.

The structural system of the building consists of a black roof slab supported on two slender columns of the same color anchored to the ground. Under this roof, which looks like a large table, were placed a number of independent blocks of different shapes, materials and colors. Sottsass has always relied on color in creating singular architectural universes, of which this house is a magnificent example. The entrance is defined by an arched door, painted bright red, which leads to an interior of serene lines that contrast with the eccentricity of the façades. On the ground floor are the common the spaces the sitting room, the dining room, the kitchen and a study with the entire floor covered in American oak, underscoring the spatial continuity. The sitting room is enclosed by a façade with large spans of glass, affording abundant views and light.

So as not to cut off the interior from the outside environment, no curtains were used in the windows of the house. Nonetheless, to avoid glare, the differences in height and size of the blocks that make up the building ensure that all rooms are shaded: the sitting room, for example, is protected by the shadow cast by the body of the bedroom. The stairway to the first floor is also of oak, with white-painted tubular metal banisters. This level was reserved

THE SLOPE OF THE LOT WAS RESOLVED BY BUILDING A LARGE PLATFORM UPON WHICH THE HOUSE SITS

Olabuenaga House

通向二楼的楼梯也是橡木制成的，并装有涂白漆的金属栏杆。二层的空间用作卧室，每间卧室都有配有独立的浴室，分别以羊毛地毯和白色瓷砖铺设地面。

大多数室内陈设，例如起居室和餐室的桌椅，都是由索特萨斯亲自设计的，而厨房设备和书房的书架是则是专属这栋别墅的独特设计。它们的颜色都注意与别墅立面保持一致。

for the bedrooms, each with its own bathroom. The floor is covered with wool carpeting, interrupted at the bathrooms, which are finished in small white ceramic tiles.

Most of the furnishings-the sitting room and dining room tables for instance-were also designed by Sottsass. The kitchen furnishings and the bookshelves in the study were designed specifically for the project. The colors are the same as those of the façades.

每个房间采用的材料、壁板和色彩都各不相同，功能区的划分从房子外部就能一目了然。南向立面就能很好地说明这一点，起居室完全被包围在玻璃墙体之中，而属于卧室的部分则在厚重的白墙上开有方形大玻璃窗。

As each room was built with different materials, sidings and colors, the differentiation between the domestic functions of the spaces can be seen from outside. A good example of this is the south façade, where the sitting room is entirely glassed-in and the bedroom has square windows cut out of a solid white-painted enclosure.

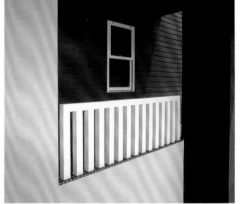

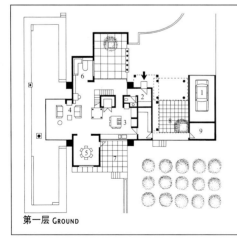

第一层 GROUND

1、车库	1. Garage
2、入口	2. Entrance
3、厨房	3. Kitchen
4、起居室	4. Sitting room
5、餐厅	5. Dining room
6、卫生间	6. Toilet
7、阳台	7. Terrace
8、庭院	8. Courtyard
9、工作间	9. Workshop

针对这项工程，放着一整套无线电通迅设施的架子以及厨房中心的临时用餐区都采用黑色漆木设计。这些元素在柔和的室内氛围中显得非常突出。

The shelves, which hold a collection of radios, and the centerpiece of the kitchen, serving as an improvised dining space, were designed in black-painted wood specifically for the project. Both elements stand out in an interior of soft shades.

建筑师：埃托里·索特萨斯
合作方：约翰纳·格拉温得
建造时间：1998 年
地址：美国 夏威夷 毛伊岛
总面积：249 平方米
摄影：安蒂因·普罗尔

Architect: Ettore Sottsass

Collaborator: Johanna Grawunder

Built: 1998

Location: Maui, Hawai, United States

Gross floor area: 2,680 sq. ft.

Photography: Undine Pröhl

扎哈·哈迪德建筑事务所 Zaha Hadid Architects

沙龙

德国沃尔夫斯堡镇议会和昆斯特艺术博物馆，委托扎哈·哈迪德建筑室在博物馆内恢复一个挑空空间以及一间大厅。哈迪德领导的团队在该市同时建造的还有一座科学技术中心，从它身上多少可以预见到博物馆的建筑风格。

在建造期间，博物馆并未对这两个空间提出具体要求，它们现在分别是两层高的展览馆和二层毗连着商店和咖啡馆的大厅。展览馆近期曾举办过摄影展览、小型绘画展和教育研习会。采用包厢式设计的大厅具有书籍查询、音像放映和酒吧等功能。

起初，展览馆准备利用属于阿尔瓦·阿尔托文化中心音乐图书馆的一处附属部分，监管会否决了这项提议后，该地又被划回博物馆所有。建筑师试图把这里变成一个灵活、动态的多功能中心，在入口处设立一个相对独立的区域，它可以进一步变成面向公共服务的空间，从而使展览馆与外界环境紧密相连。

扎哈·哈迪德的设计意图是建立展览馆、大厅及外部环境之间的联系。她把所剩区域设计成一个具有多种功能的单一空间，既可以举办模特表演和美术作品展览，还可以作为会客室、礼堂、酒吧、音乐厅或迪斯科舞厅。该项工程被称为"英国之声"，表明这里是一个集合了谈话、休闲、听音乐、用餐等多种功能的沙龙。

THE FIRST EXHIBITION IN THIS SPACE REMODELLED BY ZAHA HADID WAS DEDICATED TO WORK FROM HER OWN STUDIO

这个由扎哈·哈迪德重新规划的空间首次展出的展品就是她自己的创作。

The Kunstmuseum and the town council of Wolfsburg, Germany, commissioned Zaha Hadid to reconvert a double space and one of the lobbies in this art museum. The team headed by Hadid is also building a center dedicated to science and new technologies in the same city, so the work on this building was to anticipate the architecture of the museum complex. At the time of construction, no specific function was assigned to two of the spaces created: a double-height gallery and a lobby on the first floor which adjoins the shop and café. Until recently, the former space had held photography exhibitions, small presentations of drawings and an educational workshop. The lobby, in the form of a balcony, served for book consulting, video screenings and as an extension of the bar.

Initially, the gallery was to house an addition to a music library belonging to the Alvar Aalto cultural center, but when the administration rejected the proposal, the space was ceded to the museum. The institution sought to become a flexible, multifunctional and dynamic center, and accordingly kept an entrance area independent from the gallery with the option of transforming it later into a space for experimentation with public functions. With a close connection to the outside environment.

Zaha Hadid's intention was thus to create a link between the gallery, the lobby and the exterior. She converted the remaining areas into a single space which accommodates different functions: it is at the same time an exhibition space for models, drawings and paintings, a gathering point for the users of the complex; a waiting room; an auditorium; a bar; a concert hall and a discotheque. The project's name, the "English voice" lounge, refers to the combination of activities for which the new area is suited: talking, relaxing, listening, drinking, sitting, dreaming and eating.

The Lounge

墙壁和地面上铺设的木板赋予整个空间以连贯性，室内陈设是由哈迪德亲自设计的。她在展览馆的首次展览中展出了自己的建筑素描和模型。

The continuity of the space was attained by covering the walls and floors in wood. The furnishings were designed by the architects themselves, who also inaugurated the space with an exhibition of selected drawings and models from their own projects.

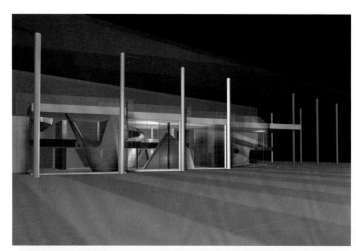

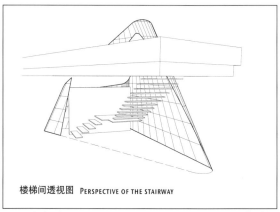

楼梯间透视图 PERSPECTIVE OF THE STAIRWAY

电脑制作的透视图 COMPUTER-GENERATED PERSPECTIVES

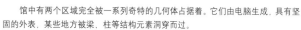

馆中有两个区域完全被一系列奇特的几何体占据着。它们由电脑生成，具有坚固的外表，某些地方被梁、柱等结构元素洞穿而过。

A series of bodies of peculiar geometry occupy the two areas of the project. The volumes, generated from computer studies, have solid enclosures perforated in some cases by structural elements such as columns or beams.

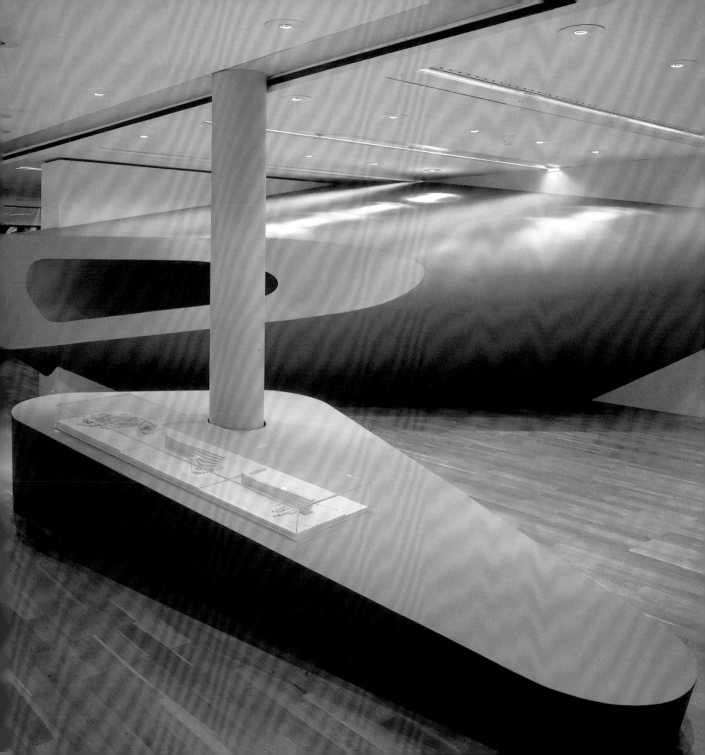

这些不规则的圆锥体从不同的方向进行切割，电脑将展示切割形成的表面。水平方向的平面图可以用来制作图纸和模型，而垂直方向的则可用于影像和幻灯展示。

The cones are irregular and cut in different directions. The resulting shapes provide display surfaces; the horizontals serve for plans and models, and the verticals for video and slide projections.

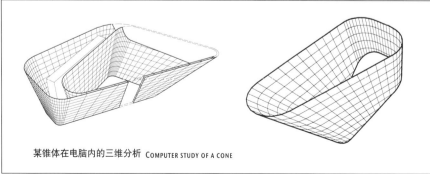

某锥体在电脑内的三维分析 COMPUTER STUDY OF A CONE

建筑师：扎哈·哈迪德建筑事务所

合作方：伍迪 · K．T．姚、乔治·斯托杰诺夫

建造时间：2001 年

地点：德国 沃尔夫斯堡

总面积：700 平方米

摄影：海伦·比奈特

Architects: Zaha Hadid Architects

Collaborators: Woody K. T. Yao and Djordje Stojanovic

Built: 2001

Location: Wolfsburg, Germany

Gross floor area: 7,526 sq. ft.

Photography: Hélène Binet

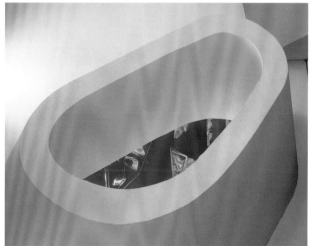

室内陈设品包括各种形状、材质的元素，它们随意的造型令使用者可以自由地运用，把它们当作桌子、沙发、床或者凳子。这种灵活的设计使每一个人都产生了无尽的遐想。

The furnishings comprise elements of varying shapes and materials. Their loosely defined geometry allows the user to use them freely: as a table, a sofa, a bed or a stool. This flexibility also fosters endless activities, according to the whims of each person.

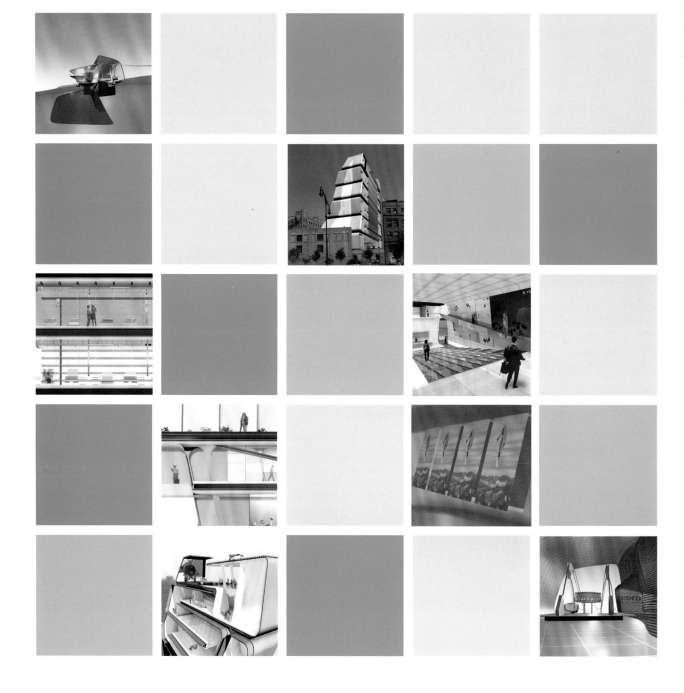

计 划 项 目
PROJECTS

李瑟建筑事务所 Leeser Architecture

眼球工作室

东曼哈顿的工业老区切尔西现已成为纽约艺术世界的中心。随着时间的推移，最具声望的艺术画廊都迁移到这个满是修车厂和仓库的地区。在这样的环境之中，眼球工作室组织了一次设计科技艺术博物馆的比赛，李瑟建筑事务所以其综合性的设计一举获胜。他们的设计使展品与展览之间、与参观者之间不再有传统意义上、泾渭分明的界线。这座博物馆在设想中是一个形态可变的空间，某些部分的地板可以方便地移走或重新装上。其中讨论区就是如此，它的地板可以根据各种需要重新组合成坡道、楼梯或者阶梯式座位。这座建筑物所有的表层部分，包括墙壁、地面以及天花板，都采用嵌板式设计，便于将展览用的投影仪、电脑和其它控件置于暗处。

这座博物馆在设想中是一个可变形的空间，某些部分的地板可以方便地移走或重新装上。

THE MUSEUM WAS CONCEIVED AS A RESHAPABLE SPACE IN WHICH SOME OF THE FLOOR SECTIONS CAN BE REMOVED AND REFITTED QUITE EASILY

The formerly industrial Chelsea neighborhood in east Manhattan has become the center of New York's artistic world. Over time the most prestigious galleries have moved to this area of small garage and warehouse buildings. Amid these surroundings, the Eyebeam Atelier organization held a competition for the construction of a new museum of art and technology, won by Leeser Architecture with a complex project that blurs the traditional frontiers between production and exhibition, between the work and the viewer.

The museum was conceived as a reshapable space in which some of the floor sections can be removed and refitted quite easily. A good example of this is the forum, where the floor can be converted into a ramp, a stairway or tiered seating to suit the needs of the moment. In addition, all the surfaces that comprise the building walls, floors and ceilings are made of panels which conceal complete fittings with projectors, computers and other control units, and thus can be used as display supports.

Eyebeam Atelier

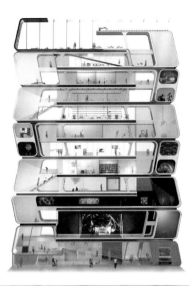

建筑师：李瑟建筑事务所
地点：美国 纽约
客户：眼球工作室

Architect: Leeser Architecture
Location: New York, USA
Client: Eyebeam Atelier

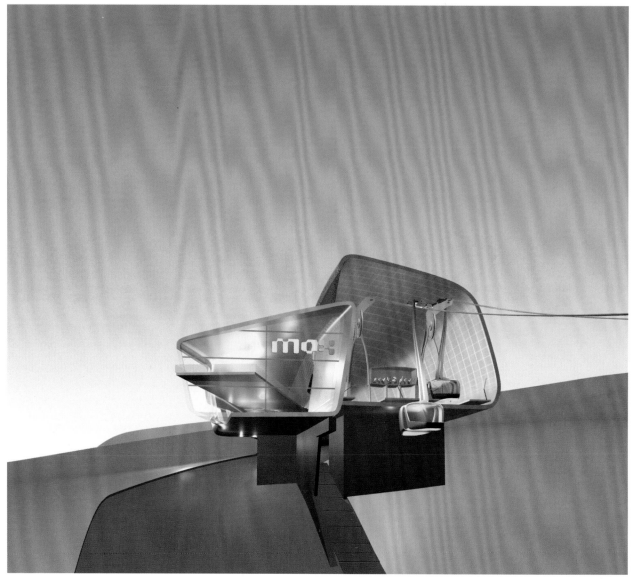

兰·威尔逊建筑文化事务所
LWPAC, Lang Wilson Practice in Architecture Culture

极限文化博物馆

近年来，旅游业已成为世界上最大的行业之一，交通、休闲、文化和旅游领域的基本建设在我们身边迅猛地发展着，新的城市规划也随之产生。在这样一个背景下，形成了建立极限文化博物馆和声纳发生器空中缆车的构想。

兰·威尔逊建筑事务所将其阐释为一项视听工程，主要由一个转运站构成，其中包括一台可容纳180名乘客的缆车、博物馆、会议中心、剧场、户外礼堂和一些办公室。这些建筑空间组成一个连续、灵活的整体景观，根据季节或者活动项目可以相应增加或缩减其功能。

建筑师选择了轻质材料和预制构件，从而使高山上的工程建设变得相对容易。

这些建筑空间形成一个连续灵活的整体景观，根据季节或者活动情况可以相应增加或缩减少其功能。

ALL THE SPACES FORM A SINGLE, CONTINUOUS AND FLEXIBLE LANDSCAPE, CAPABLE OF EXPANDING OR CONTRACTING ITS USES ACCORDING TO THE SEASON OR ACTIVITIES PROGRAM

In recent years tourism has become one of the biggest industries in the world, and thus transportation, leisure, culture and tourism infrastructures have proliferated all around us and led to new urban planning projects. In this context the Museum of Extreme Culture and the Peak-to-Peak aerial cable car were conceived.

The commission received by LWPAC architects, which was to be presented in the form of an audiovisual projection, consisted of a transport station with a cable car for 180 passengers, a museum, a convention center, offices, a theater and an outdoor auditorium. All these spaces form a single, continuous and flexible landscape, capable of expanding or contracting its uses according to the season or activities program.

The architects chose light materials and prefabricated structures to facilitate and even make possible construction high up on a mountain.

Museum of Extreme Culture

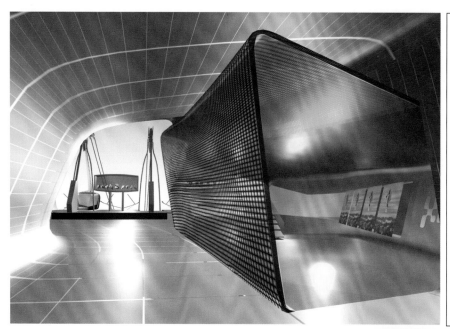

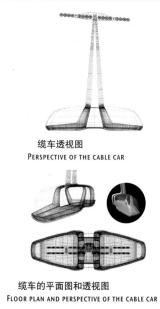

缆车透视图
PERSPECTIVE OF THE CABLE CAR

缆车的平面图和透视图
FLOOR PLAN AND PERSPECTIVE OF THE CABLE CAR

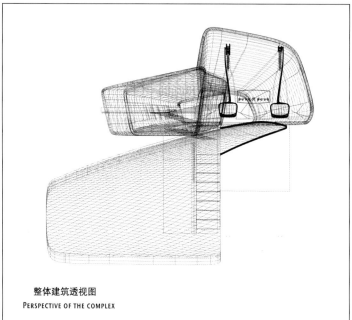

整体建筑透视图
PERSPECTIVE OF THE COMPLEX

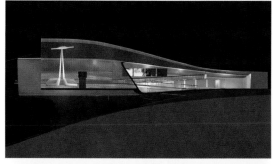

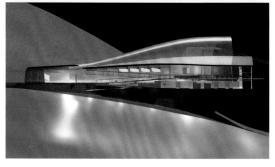

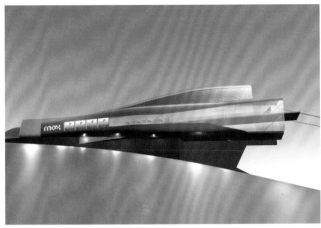

建筑师：兰·威尔逊建筑事务所
合作方：罗伯托 E & S 公司、想像与传说公司
项目时间：2002 年
总面积：1800 平方米

Architect: LWPAC, Lang Wilson Practice
in Architecture Culture
Collaborators: Roberto E&S, Envisioning & Storytelling
Project date: 2002
Gross floor area: 19.354 sq. ft.

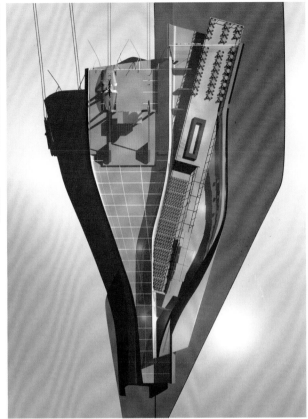

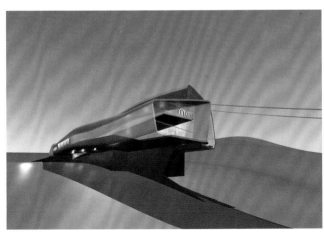

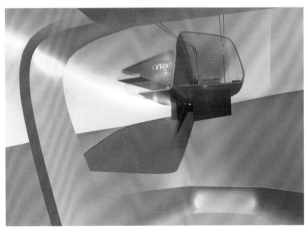

家具
FURNITURE

极繁主义家具

直切主题的一点是，这些新设计毫不犹豫地摈弃了在20世纪90年代占统治地位的含蓄和冷淡的风格。丰富的想像和感性色彩的运用，与从前的单调和简朴截然相反，这充分说明家具设计领域的新理念。简单与平淡、仿佛不可见的线条、冷漠的钢铁和玻璃以及中性白色调已经主导设计潮流将近十年，现在家具设计将要告别简约主义，取而代之的则是夸张、炫耀及经过精心构思的繁复品味。如今的家具设计是一个对社会的各种影响和变化相当敏锐的领域，而这些影响变化都直接指向引人注目的极奢主义风格，将形式主义的谨小慎微抛在一旁。现在认为极奢主义已成潮流尚为时太早，市场中许多环节仍拥戴密斯·范德罗提出的"少即是好"的原则，90年代仍有许多设计家和建筑师捍卫这个原则，并将其用于实践。不过，夸张的设计风格正在迅速扩大自己的影响，繁复和豪华又卷土重来。繁复之风带来了大量以往从不可能出现的奇形怪状。新鲜、生动和大胆的变化使现在的设计极富色彩，带给人们难以置信的愉悦感。全新的、甚至无从想象的材质也渐渐受到欢迎。这些设计毫不掩饰地展示着大胆、鲜明、自然而又极富人性的种种形态。它们无视世人的眼光和评判，公然向各种我们曾经跟从的纯正、单一的设计成规发起挑战。

Falling just short of excess, the new designs opt to shed the shyness and frigidity which ruled the nineties in favor of near-reckless abandon. Copious doses of imagination and a feeling quite the opposite of formal austerity define many of the latest proposals in furniture design. After a decade dominated by simplicity and plain, near-invisible lines, the coldness of steel and glass and the neutrality of white, a departure from minimalism arises coupled with a carefree approach to exaggeration, ostentation and a taste for well-conceived excess.

Furniture design has become a discipline open to all sorts of influences and changes affecting society, and these changes now point to a striking maximalist style, leaving behind formal subtlety and discretion.

It is early yet to speak of a generalized trend, what with numerous sectors of the market still adhering to "less is more" -defended in his day by Mies van der Rohe and championed in the nineties by designers and architects who took his words to their final consequences. Now, however, exaggeration is gaining ground apace; fatuousness and luxury are back to stay.

Exuberance materializes in uninhibited, generous and on occasion impossible shapes. Fresh, vivid and whimsical shades color the designs, and dress them in textures as pleasant as they are surprising, at the same time new, and until recently, unthinkable, materials are favored for their craftsmanship.

These designs wear their expressiveness with pride: daring, bold, spontaneous shapes abounding in personality; elements whose lines scorn the risk of experimentation and defy the rules to the point that we surrender to their sublime, genuine singularity.

Maximalist Furniture

卡柏斯方桌 Karpousi
瓦莱斯公司 Valais

萨玛罗利指纹方桌 Zamaroli Fingerprint
瓦莱斯公司 Valais

汉斯格鲁垫子 Hansgrum
迈克尔·柯尼希 Michael Koenig

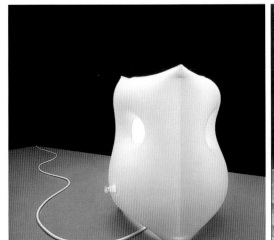

台灯 Table Light
尼克·克罗斯比 Nick Crosbie
充气用品有限公司 Inflate Ltd.

座椅 Design
马克·纽森 de Marc Newson

德鲁格格蕾丝 Droog Lacet
马塞尔·旺德斯工作室 Marcel Wanders
Studio

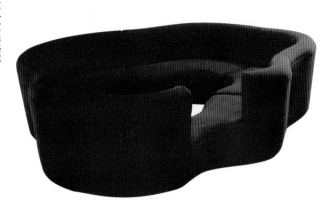

整体沙发 Omni
卡里姆·拉希德，盖尔金公司 Karim Rashid, Galerkin

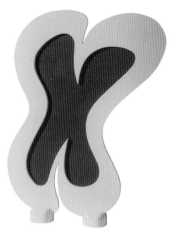

不喜爱相框 No mires
特里萨·塞普克里，苔斯公司 Teresa Sepulcre, Tes

邦姆贮物架 Bum—Bum
特里萨·塞普克里，苔斯公司 Teresa
Sepulcre，Tes

奇克休闲椅 Chiqui—Chiqui
特里萨·塞普克里，苔斯公司 Teresa
Sepulcre，Tes

沙龙椅 Lounge Chair
尼克·克罗斯比，充气用品有限公司Nick Crosbie,
Inflate Ltd

蛋形花瓶 Eggvases
马塞尔·旺德斯工作室 Marcel Wanders Studio

海绵瓶 Spongeva
马塞尔·旺德斯工作室Marcel Wanders Studio

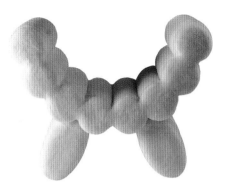

特鲁鲁椅 Tururu
特里萨·塞普克里，苔斯公司Teresa Sepulcre，Tes

航海者之巢座椅 Voyager Nest
意大利萨托里尼 Saporiti Italia

蘑菇桌 Qual Mazzolin
迪尔莫斯公司弗罗里、波托兹和达尔·蒙特·卡瑟尼Diori，Bertozzi & Fal Monte
Casoni，Kilmos

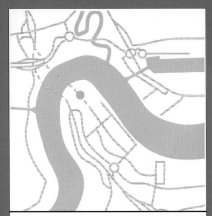

精神时空

英国 伦敦 格林威治半岛 千禧年穹顶(Millenium Dome)

扎哈·哈迪德建筑事务所

gayle@zaha-hadid.com

第 10 页

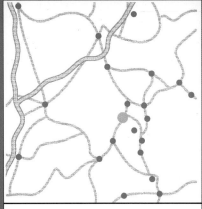

巴德埃尔斯特温泉

德国 巴德埃尔斯特 沐浴大街 (Bad Strasse) 6 号

贝尼施建筑事务所

bp@behnisch.com

第 16 页

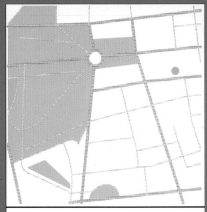

DZ 银行

德国 柏林 巴黎广场 3 号 (Pariseplatz 3)

盖瑞建筑事务所

keithm@foga.com

第 24 页

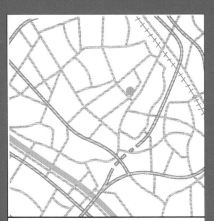

克里斯汀－拉克鲁瓦精品服装店

日本 东京都 涩谷区 猿楽町 (Sarugaku-cho) 24-4 号

卡普斯建筑事务所

elockard@caps-architects.com

第 32 页

佩克汉姆图书馆

英国 伦敦 派克汉姆山大街 (Pechham Hill Street) 122 号

阿尔索普和斯托默尔建筑事务所

alsoparchitects.com

第 38 页

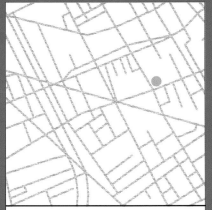

MTV 总部

美国 圣莫尼卡市 科罗拉多大道 第 26 街
(Colorado Boulevard 26th Street)

菲尔德曼和基廷联合事务所

www.fkadesign.com

第 44 页

B 煤气厂

奥地利维也纳古格拉斯大街12号 (Guglasse 12)

蓝天组事务所

www.coop-himmelblau.com

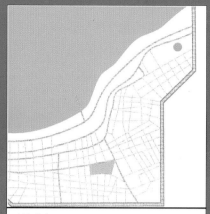

建筑学院

智利 瓦尔帕莱索市 西班牙1680大街 (Avenida Espana 1680)

兰·威尔逊建筑文化事务所

olang@lwpac.net

奥尔布薇娜格别墅

美国 夏威夷 毛伊岛 (Maui)

埃托里·索特萨斯

delgreco@sottsass.it

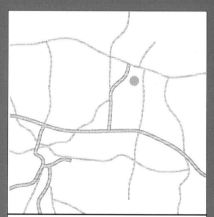

沙龙

德国 沃尔夫斯堡 保时捷街 (Porsche Strasse) 53 号

扎哈·哈迪德建筑事务所

gayle@zaha-hadid.com

眼球工作室

美国 纽约

李瑟建筑事务所

www.keeser.com

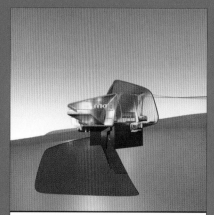

极限文化博物馆

兰·威尔逊建筑文化事务所

olang@lwpac.net

瓦格纳与克里姆特

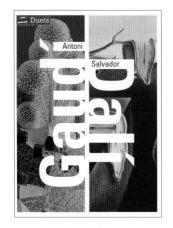

达利与高迪

格罗皮乌斯与凯利

米罗与塞尔特

赖特与欧姬芙

里特维尔德与蒙特利安

maximalism

maximalism

maximalism

maximalism

maximalism

maximalism

极繁主义建筑设计

maximalism

maximalismo

maximalism

maxim

maxim